But magic isn't easy.
My hair, with its tangles and snarls,
defies my mother's comb.
"Hold still," Mama sings.
I growl in frustration, then take a deep breath
and remind myself to be patient,
imagining what new surprise my hair will become. . . .

Tall and strong, my hair stands
like regal pine trees,
silently guarding the pristine peace
of mountainside lakes.

My hair is majestic like that.

Turning and coiling around itself,
it moves like a million ocean currents,
playfully pulling at tiny sailboats,
gently jiggling their carefully plotted paths.

My hair is mischievous like that.

Wrapped in tiny Bantu knots,
each strand tucked tight,
it's like windswept desert stone—
mighty monuments rippling across
a sandy sunset horizon.

My hair is stunning like that.

Thick and dark, it's a cloudless sky on a winter night.
Bright barrettes dance like stars—
floating flashes suspended in soft, limitless blackness.

My hair is mesmerizing like that.

Brushed and teased to rounded perfection,
it blooms like a bouquet of hydrangea blossoms
adorning the spring with splendor.

My hair is elegant like that.

Ironed flat, it's light as the autumn breeze,
carrying the fragrance of fresh-cut hay,
ripe apples, and dried pine needles,
all mingling softly under my nose.

My hair is whimsical like that.

Braided, it dangles gently around my face
like long vines tumbling from a garden trellis—
woven tightly, swaying loosely,
flexible, but unbreakable.

My hair is strong like that.

Piled high, it gathers together
like billowing thunderclouds
threatening to break loose in a sudden storm,
releasing a cascade of relief and revival.

My hair is fresh like that.

So when Mama's fingers finish casting their spell
and she sits back with a satisfied sigh, patting and smoothing,
anticipation stirs my stomach
like lightning bugs in a glass jar
eager to escape.

I can be anything . . .

. . . a resplendent queen of the mountains,

a fearless explorer of infinite stars,

a powerful warrior unleashed!

Magic isn't easy, but it is always worth this moment.
"What do you think?" Mama asks.
"It's fire," I say, slowly smiling as I behold
the most brilliant version of myself yet.

My hair is magic like that.